# THE POSEIDON ADVENTURE

The afternoon sky is grey. The sea is grey, too. It is very rough, with very big waves. A big ship goes up – up to the white tops of the waves – and then down, down between two big waves. The ship's name is *S.S. Poseidon*. The *Poseidon*'s captain is standing on the bridge of the ship. He is looking out over the sea. He can see only the big waves, the grey sea. Three officers are on the bridge with him.

"This rough sea is bad," the captain says. "The *Poseidon* is an old ship. We have hundreds of people on the ship."

The officers don't answer. They are looking at the rough waves, too.

"Please!" A small boy is standing behind the captain. "Please, Captain" he says again.

The captain looks at him. "Who ar you?" the captain asks.

"Can I see your ship? Can I see the engine room, and the kitchens and the decks, too? Please, can I?" the boy asks.

"The waves are big today, and the ship is going up and down. The water is coming over the decks," the captain answers. "Are you afraid

"No! I'm not afraid! Take me down to the engine room, please!"

"What's your name?" the captain asks.

"Robin. Robin Shelby."

"OK, Robin," the captain says. "Come with me."

They go down the stairs to the next deck. Robin asks questions and the captain answers him.

"The bridge is at the top of the ship, isn't it?"

"Yes. It's over the top deck."

"What's in there?"

"The dining room. Those stairs go down to the kitchens."

"And what's the next door? Is it the door of the engine room?"

"No, it isn't. The engine room is under us. It's at the bottom of the ship."

"Susan! Susan!" Robin says to his sister. She is in their room.

"Susan, the captain showed me the ship. I saw the engine room at the bottom of the ship, and four or five decks, and . . . What are you doing?"

"I'm dressing. I'm going to go to the party tonight."

"What party?" Robin asks.

"Tonight is New Year's Eve! There's a big party in the dining room."

Manny and Belle Rosen are sitting on deck. Manny is reading a book. Belle is looking at the sea. The tops of the waves are white.

A man is running along the deck. Belle says to Manny, "Mr Martin run on deck every day, doesn't he?"

Mr Martin is in front of them now.

"Hello, Mr Martin," Belle says.

"Good afternoon," Mr Martin answers. "The sea is rough, isn't it? But we're going to arrive soon. And you're going to see your family."

"Yes. Our daughter's little boy – Peter. He can walk now. I'm happy: we're going to see him soon."

"That's nice," Mr Martin says.

The night sky is black and the waves are high now. On the bridge, the captain looks at the sea. He doesn't speak.

Everybody is at the party now. Nonnie and her brother Teddy are singing. There is a tall Christmas tree in the dining room. There are letters across the room: HAPPY NEW YEAR.

The people are sitting at small tables. They are eating and drinking. People are dancing, too.

"Are you going to dance, Mr Martin?" Belle asks.

"Oh, no," he answers. "I never dance."

"But you're not old!" she says. "Dance with one of these pretty girls."

"But I can't dance!" he answers.

The captain is sitting at his table now. Frank Scott is beside him. Linda and Mike Rogo are at the table too.

A man is sitting beside Susan Shelby at the next table. "Come and dance with me," he says to her.

Susan doesn't answer. She is looking across the room at Scott.

The man speaks to her again. "Come and dance with me, please."

"Oh," Susan says. "Oh, OK."

An officer comes into the dining room and goes to the captain's table. "Can you come to the bridge, please, Captain?" the officer asks.

The captain stands up. "Yes," he says. "I'm coming."

On the bridge, a voice is coming
over the radio.

".. . rough seas near Crete,"
the voice is saying. "High waves
are putting ships in danger.
*Boats and ships are in danger
near Crete . . ."*

"We're very near Crete," the
captain says to his men. "I'm
afraid of these high waves."

Suddenly, one of the officers shouts,
"Look! Look at that wave!"

A high wall of water is moving
across the sea. It is very near the
*Poseidon.* It is moving very quickly.

"Oh, no!" the captain shouts.
He is afraid. "That wave! It's
five miles across . . . it's coming
very quickly! It's going to hit us!
It's going to hit the ship!"

In the dining room, everybody is
singing and dancing.

"Happy New Year!" Nonnie shouts.

Happy voices answer her:
"Happy New Year!"
"Happy New Year!"

Manny Rosen takes Belle in his arms.
"Happy New Year, my dear," he
says. He kisses her.

Linda kisses Rogo, and she kisses
Scott, too.

Everybody dances.

6

Suddenly, the big
wave hits the *Poseidon*.
The old ship goes to
the top of the wave.
But the wave is very,
very big. The ship
is turning. *It is
turning over* . . .

People in the dining
room fall to the floor.
The food and drink
falls off the tables.
Everybody is shouting.
Their heads hit the
floor. Hands hold
the legs of chairs
and tables. But they
can't hold them.
They fall. The ship
is turning, turning . . .

The bottom of the ship comes out of
the black water. The *Poseidon* is
upside down in the sea! The ship's
propellers are out of the water.
The propellers aren't moving now.

The floor of the dining room is now
above the people's heads. They
look up, and they see tables upside
down. People are holding on to
the tables. But they can't hold them.
A man falls.

Scott stands up. He looks round
the room: clothes, shoes, chairs,
arms and legs, the bodies of dead
people. One or two people are on
their feet. He sees Martin.

Martin is putting his coat over the
body of a dead woman beside him.

"Are you hurt, Martin?" Scott asks.

"No, I'm OK. I'm not hurt,"
Martin answers. "The ship's upside
down!"

"Yes!"

"Susan! Susan!" Robin is running
round the room. He is shouting.

"Robin, are you hurt?"
Scott takes Robin's hand.

"I'm OK, but I can't see Susan,"
Robin answers.

"Help! Please help me!"
That is Susan's voice.
Robin and Scott go to her.

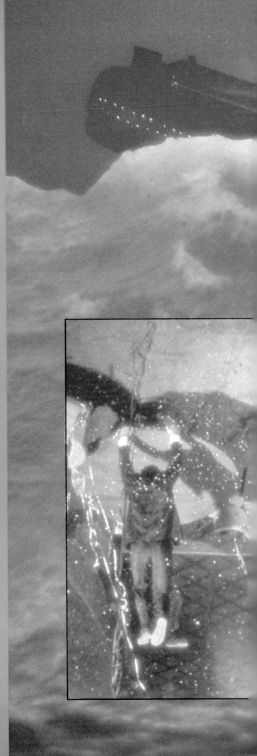

Belle is shouting now. "Manny, Manny, you're hurt! Your head!"

"It's not bad, my dear. It's OK," Manny answers.

One of the officers stands up. "Please stay in this room, everybody," he says. "The captain is going to come and help us. Stay in this room, please!"

"But the ship is upside down," Sco says. "The captain was on the bridge. The top of the ship is under water. He is dead now. His officers are dea too. Nobody is going to come and he us. We can't stay in this room."

"What can we do?" Rogo asks. Rogo and Linda aren't hurt.

"Climb up," Martin answers him. "We can climb up and get out of the bottom of the ship."

"Climb up?!" Rogo shouts.
"Look at that!"

Everybody looks up at the floor high above their heads.

"There are three or four decks," Rogo says. "We can't do that."

"We can," Scott says. "This ship is going down. The water is going to come into this room soon."

"Please, everybody! Stay in this room!" the officer shouts.

"What's on the next deck?" Linda asks.

"The kitchens," Robin answers. "There are the kitchens, and then the engine rooms. We can get out by the propellers. The bottom of the ship is not very thick near the propellers."

"What are you saying?" Rogo says. His voice is nasty. "You're only a child."

"The captain showed me the ship this afternoon," Robin answers. "I can take you!"

"But we can't get up to the next deck, can we?" Rogo says.

Nobody speaks. Then Martin says, "The Christmas tree! We can lift the tree, and then climb up it. We can get to the next deck."

"Yes!" Scott shouts. "Quickly! Come and help us, everybody. It's heavy."

They all go and help Scott and Martin.

"One . . . two . . . three . . . *lift!*" Scott shouts. The tree is very heavy. But they lift it, and it moves.

"Now," Scott says. "We climb up. Robin, you can climb can't you?"

"OK – we climb up the tree. *Then* what do we do?" Rogo asks.

"We go on up. Up to the next deck, and the next."

"We can't climb up the tree in these long party dresses," Linda says to the women. "Take them off."

"What?!" Rogo shouts.

"Oh, give me your shirt then," she says.

"OK, Susan, you go next," Scott says.

Susan takes off her long dress. She goes up the tree.

"Are you going to come too?" Scott asks the Rosens.

"I'm going to stay here," Belle says. "I can't climb up the tree – I'm old and fat."

"Yes, you can," Manny says. "Come on! I'm behind you."

Martin speaks to the people in the room.

"Please, everybody, come with us. The water is going to come into this room very soon. The ship is going down. The captain is dead; nobody's going to help us."

"We're going to stay here," they answer. "You can't get out."

Then Martin sees Nonnie. She is on the floor beside her brother. His eyes are shut and he isn't moving.

"Oh please, Teddy," she is saying to him. "Open your eyes. Stand up, Teddy, and come with me. Help me, Teddy!"

Martin speaks to her. "Miss ... Leave him now, and come with me."

"Leave him? But ... I can't leave him. He's my family ... I've got nobody ..."

"What's your name?"

"Nonnie."

"Nonnie," Martin says, "your brother is dead."

She doesn't speak. Martin takes her hand and she stands up. They walk slowly to the bottom of the tree. She climbs up.

Nine people are at the top of the tree now: Rogo and Linda, Manny and Belle, Susan and Robin, Nonnie, Martin and Scott. Scott turns to the people in the room under them. He is going to speak to them again.

But suddenly a big explosion shakes the ship. The explosion is under the dining room. The water is coming in – very quickly! Soon the room is going to be full of water. It is round the people's legs. They run to the bottom of the tree. But the water moves around the bottom of the tree and the tree falls. Now nobody can get out.

The nine people at the top move on.
In front of them, they see the door
to the kitchens. But what is coming
from behind the door?

"Smoke!" Robin says. "There's a
fire in the kitchens!"

"We can't open the door," Rogo says.
"The smoke is thick. It's very
dangerous. We can't go on."

"I'm going to open it," Scott says.
He pulls the heavy door. It is very
hot. His face is red; he pulls and
pulls. The door opens suddenly.
Scott runs into the thick grey smoke.

"OK," he shouts. "You can come
through the door. Run!"

Everybody runs through the door
into the kitchens. Nonnie sees the
bodies; she puts her hands over her
face. Martin puts his arm round her.

"What's at the end of the kitchens?"
Scott asks Robin.

"A passage," Robin answers, "and
then stairs. The engine room is at the
top of the stairs."

They run through the thick smoke.
They get to the passage at the end
of the room. But ... look! The
passage is under water. They can't
get to the stairs.

"What can we do now?" Susan
asks. "We can't get to the next deck.
I'm afraid ..."

Scott puts his arm round the girl.
"I'm going to find a way," he says.

"There's a shaft," Robin says
suddenly. "I saw it. The shaft goes
from the top of the ship to the
bottom. There's a way into the
shaft from the decks. We can
find it."

Martin sees a very small door in
the wall. "Is this it?" he asks.
"It's only a thin pipe!"

"Yes," Robin says. "It's an air
pipe. It goes to the shaft. We can
go through it."

"I can't go through that pipe!"
Belle says. "You can; you're thin.
But I'm fat! I can't!"

"It's the only way," Robin answers.

Suddenly Linda shouts, "The
water's coming up! Quickly! Get
into the pipe, everybody!"

Robin and Susan move slowly
through the thin pipe. Nonnie is
behind them.

"Help me, Manny, help me! Pull me!" Belle shouts. The water is round their feet now. Manny pulls her, and slowly she, too, moves along the pipe.

Rogo and Scott are in front. They find the shaft. It is very high. They look up and down. At the bottom they can see the black water.

"Look up!" Rogo shouts. "You're not going to fall."

But Nonnie is looking down at the black water. It is moving up quickly now. "I'm afraid!" she says. "I can't move. I'm going to fall."

"No, you're not. I'm behind you," Martin says. "Go on, Nonnie. Put one foot up. And again. Good."

At the top of the shaft, they are
in a passage.

"Only one deck now," Robin says.
"I'm going to find the stairs."
He goes along the passage.

Scott and Rogo help Belle and
Manny out of the shaft.

Suddenly, two big explosions
shake the ship again.

"Quickly!" Martin shouts. "The
ship is going down. The water
is coming into this passage.
Look! The stairs are this
way."

"But Robin's that way!" Susan says.

They look along the long passage. They can't see the small boy. But they *can* see a river of water! It is moving along the passage.

"Robin!" Susan shouts. She is afraid. "Find Robin! He isn't here!"

"I'm going to find him," Scott says,

"Get up the stairs, everybody!" Martin shouts.

"I can't go! I can't leave Robin!" Susan says.

The water is moving quickly. It is high now. Suddenly, Susan sees Robin and Scott. They are running along the passage. The black river is behind them. They get near the stairs. The water is round their bodies. It is pulling the boy down. He can't move. Scott holds the child.

Rogo pushes Susan up the stairs. "Go on, Susan!" he shouts. "Robin's OK. Scott's holding him."

The men lift Robin and push him up the stairs. Then they climb up quickly.

At the top of the stairs, Scott looks round. "Is everybody OK?" he asks.

"Yes, we're OK," Belle answers. "What do we do now?"

"This passage goes to the engine room," Robin says.

"But look!" Martin says. "It's under water."

Nobody speaks. Everybody is afraid now. Can they go on?

"Rogo, you've got a rope, haven't you?" Scott asks slowly.

"Yes. I've got a rope. But—"

"Tie the rope round me," Scott says.

"What are you going to do?" Susan asks.

"Tie the rope round me. I'm going to swim along the passage under the water. The engine room is above us. The water isn't in the engine room. I'm going to swim through and get up into the engine room."

"Please, Scott!" Susan holds his arm. "That's very dangerous. You can't do it."

He doesn't answer her. He says, "Rogo, you hold the end of the rope. I'm going to get into the engine room. Then I'm going to pull on the rope. Then everybody can swim through."

"*I* can swim through," Belle says suddenly. Everybody looks at her. "I'm old and fat now, but I was a very good swimmer. I can go."

"You *were* a very good swimmer, my dear," Manny says. "But you were young then. You can't do it now. Scott can do it. He's young."

"Hold the end of the rope," Scott says. He jumps into the water.

They wait. Susan shuts her eyes. She is very afraid. Nobody speaks. They wait, but Scott doesn't pull the rope.

"He can't stay under the water," Susan says. "Pull the rope! Pull him up!"

The men pull the rope . . . but it doesn't move!

Belle takes off her shoes. Manny puts his arms round her quickly. Then she jumps into the black water.

nder the water, she swims quickly
ong the rope. Suddenly she sees
cott. The rope is round a pipe.
is holding Scott; he can't move.
elle swims up to him. Quickly she
oves the rope. She helps Scott, and
hey swim up out of the water into
he engine room.

They can't speak. There are fires in
he engine room. Bodies are lying
n the ground around them. Then
elle says, "You see, Mr Scott,
am a good swimmer."

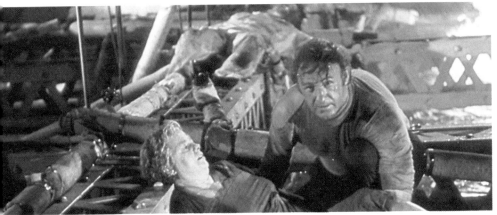

"Thank you, Belle," Scott says.
"I . . . Belle? Are you OK?"

Belle is standing with her hands
n her heart. Her face is white.
"My . . . my heart . . ." she says.
Suddenly, she falls.

"Belle!" Scott shouts. He runs
o her and lifts her head. "You're
oing to be OK, Belle," he says,
"Hold on, hold on".

"No, no," Belle says. "That swim . . .
my heart . . . I'm not young now . . ."

Her voice is very quiet. Her fingers
are holding a medallion round
her neck. Slowly she takes off the
medallion. "Give this medallion
to Manny," she says. "It's for Peter,
our daughter's little boy. I'm not
going to see him now."

Scott takes the medallion.
He holds Belle in his arms.
She doesn't speak or move again.

"Oh, no," Scott says. "She's
dead . . ." Slowly he pulls the rope.

"He's pulling the rope!" Rogo shouts. "They're there! We can swim through now. Come on, everybody!" He jumps into the water.

"I can't go," Nonnie says suddenly. "Leave me here. I . . . I can't swim."

"I'm not going to leave you," Martin says. "Hold on to me. I can take you. Don't be afraid, Nonnie. I'm not going to leave you here."

In the engine room, Rogo helps Manny out of the water. Manny sees his wife on the ground. "You're here, my dear!" he says. "You're here, and . . . Belle! Are you OK, Belle?" He runs to her.

"She's here," Scott says to him very quietly. "I owe my life to her. You too – you owe your lives to her.

Her heart . . ."

Manny takes his dead wife in his arms. Nobody speaks. They can't help him.

Then Scott says, "Belle's dead. W can't do anything for her. We're going to go on." He turns to Manny "Come on," he says quietly.

"No," Manny answers. "My place is here – with her. I'm going to stay here."

"Look, Manny," Scott says. "Thi is from Belle." He holds up the medallion. "Give this medallion to Peter. Your place is with your family. Leave Belle now, and come with us."

Manny kisses Belle's face, and stands up slowly.

They move on through the engine
room. There is a long, high catwalk
across the room.

"Look!" Robin shouts. "Up there!
That's the door to the propeller
shaft. I can see it now." He helps
Susan up to the catwalk.

"Hold on, everybody," Scott shouts.
"The catwalk is dangerous. It's
very high."

Under them they can see fire and
smoke and the black water. They
hear a big explosion. It shakes
the ship.

"Hold on!" Scott shouts again.

"I'm afraid," Linda says. "Help
me, please, Rogo."

"You're OK," Rogo answers. "I'm
going in front of you."

Suddenly, the ship moves to one
side. They hold the side of the catwalk
quickly. But Linda can't hold on.
She falls suddenly, down through the
smoke and fire, down and down
into the black water.

"Linda, Linda, my Linda . . ." Rogo
shouts.

But Linda is dead.

AAAGGHH!

SSSSSS

Suddenly, there is a new noise. Scott turns and looks up – there is a cloud of hot steam. The steam is coming from a big pipe above their heads. It is coming out very quickly, and it is moving across a small door.

"Look at that steam!" Scott shouts.

"But that's the door!" Robin says. "That's the door to the propeller shaft. And the steam . . . it's very hot . . we can't get through it!"

They can see a big wheel on the pipe. The wheel shuts off the steam. But it's very high. And the steam is very, very hot.

"Belle is dead," Scott says very quietly. "Linda is dead. And we are very near. That's the door to the propeller shaft."

Suddenly, Scott jumps. He jumps across from the catwalk, and he holds the big wheel with one hand. The hot steam is in his face, on his arms, over his body. Nobody can get to him. He can't get across to the catwalk again. Slowly, slowly, he turns the wheel. He is stopping the steam.

"Go on!" Scott shouts. "You can get through the door now. Rogo, take them through. *Go on!*"

27

AAAAGCCHH!

Nobody moves. They are looking at Scott. He is holding on, holding on . . . but he can't. With a shout, Scott falls down, down into the black water.

Then Susan shouts, again and again, "Scott! Scott! Scott!" She turns and goes down. "I'm going to help him!" She runs quickly along the catwalk.

"No! Susan! It's dangerous . . . you can't go down there!" Robin shouts. Robin and Martin run and get her. They hold her.

"You can't go down, Susan," Martin says. "Scott's dead. We owe our lives to him; we can go on. But he's dead." Then he shouts to Rogo, "Go on, Rogo! Take everybody through. You can do it!"

"OK," Rogo answers. "I'm going in front."

He moves slowly across to the door and opens it. The six people go through the small door. They are under the bottom of the ship now. The propeller shaft is small. They look around.

"Well, what do we do now?" Rogo asks. "There isn't a way out of here."

"No," Robin answers, "but the bottom of the ship isn't very thick near the propellers. We can—"

"Quiet!" Martin says suddenly. "I can hear something."

Nobody speaks. They hear a small noise. The noise comes again. Then . . .

"Footsteps!" Nonnie shouts. "I can hear footsteps! Somebody's out there!"

"Yes, yes! Somebody is walking across the bottom of the ship," Susan says. "Make a noise – make a big noise!"

Rogo and Martin hit the bottom of the ship above their heads. They hit it and hit it, again and again.

"Wait," Rogo says. They wait, but they can't hear anything now.

"They can't hear us," Susan says. "They're going away."

"Go on, go on," Manny says. He hits the bottom of the ship too. The three men make a very loud noi

Suddenly, they hear an answer. Nobody moves. *Tap tap tap* – the noise comes again.

"There *is* somebody there!" Rogo says. *Tap tap tap* – he hits the place above his head. They hear footsteps again. People are moving above the The taps are near; they are above them now. There are noises and voices.

"We're OK! They're going to save us!" Everybody is shouting.

They look up at the bottom of the ship over their heads. They see smoke, and a hot, red place.

"They're cutting through it!" Robin shouts. "They're cutting a hole in the ship!"

Then suddenly the yellow sun shines through the hole on their dirty faces. A man's face looks down at them.

"Who's there?" he asks. "Only six of you?"

"Yes," Martin answers quietly. "Only six."

They can hear the noise of a helicopter. Then men help them out through the hole. They get into the helicopter: Nonnie and Martin, Robin and Susan, Rogo. Manny stands and looks down into the hole again. In his hand is Belle's medallion. Then he turns and gets into the helicopter.

**Exercises**

*1* Look at pages 1 and 2 and answer these questions.
   a) What is the name of the ship?
   b) Who is the little boy?
   c) Where does the ship's captain take him?

   Look at pages 5 and 6 and answer these questions.
   d) Where is everybody?
   e) What is everybody doing?
   f) Who is singing?
   g) What does the officer on the bridge see?

*2* Read pages 7–10, and look at the pictures. Now write down these sentences and p
   in the missing words.
   The big *a)*— hits the *Poseidon.* In the dining room, food and drink falls off the *b*
   The people *c)*— to the floor. They *d)*— hold the legs of the tables and chairs. The
   old ship is *e)*—; it turns *f)*— in the water. The floor of the dining room is now *g)*
   the people's heads.

*3* Read pages 17 and 18 and answer these questions.
   a) What is coming from behind the door?
   b) What does Scott do?
   c) Why is the door hot?
   d) Why does Nonnie put her hands over her face?

*4* Read pages 23 and 24. Write down these sentences. Choose the right word.
   a) The passage to the engine room is *over/under/behind* water.
   b) Scott is going to *swim/walk/run* through the water.
   c) "*Make/tie/leave* the rope round me," Scott says.
   d) "I was a very *young/fat/good* swimmer," Belle says.
   e) Belle takes *off/over/up* her shoes.
   f) Then Belle *walks/jumps/eats* into the black water.

*5* Look at page 25. Answer these questions.
   a) "He's pulling the rope!"
      i) Who says this?
      ii) Who is he talking to?
      iii) Who is he talking about?
   b) "I owe my life to her."
      i) Who says this?
      ii) Who is he talking to?
      iii) Who is he talking about?